The Little Lambs
Costume Party Surprise

Illustrations by José-Luis Macias S.
Original story by M.C. Suigne
Retold by Linda L. Booth

Once a year Maggie and her friends organize a wonderful costume party. But there is still much work to be done. The party takes place in town, and everyone joins in. There are prizes for the most original and the best made costumes. The children have worked very hard this year, and the big day is finally here. Cindy is dressed up as a fairy princess, and her little sister is a witch. Jason and Tommy are disguised as a bull, and they think they'll win first prize.

Everyone starts into town for the party. Jason and Tommy walk ahead of the others, but they can't see very well under their costume. Look out . . . !

Jason and Tommy tumble down a little hill. They aren't hurt, but their bull mask is bent and needs fixing. "You can catch up with us in town," Paul says, with a wave of his hat.

The party is a great success! The children look splendid in their costumes, and they begin parading past the judges. Who will win first prize? What is keeping Jason and Tommy?

Hurrah! Jason and Tommy have repaired their mask, and
suddenly appear in front of the judges. Everyone is delighted.
"Now they look just like a real bull," Maggie exclaims. The jury
is impressed with the originality of the costume. No question
about who will win....

The bull, of course, wins first prize! But it's strange — the winners don't seem too excited about the presentation. While everyone is admiring the crown, a little girl dressed as a bee discovers Jason and Tommy hiding behind the curtain. "But who is under the bull costume?" she asks anxiously.

A jury member removes the bull's mask, and what a surprise—a
real live bull, and he's not in the best mood! Everyone runs
away. "Disqualified!" shouts the jury. The children are angry.
"What cheaters those boys are," they say.

The bull safely penned in, our little friends are content to share the first prize among themselves. Even Jason and Tommy are allowed to join in after a while. All in all, it was a wonderful costume party!

Published in the United States and simultaneously in Canada by Joshua Morris, Inc.
431 Post Road East, Westport, CT 06880
Printed in Belgium